They all gathered closer as
Great-Uncle Horace slowly
pulled back the towel. Zoe
peered inside the basket and saw
a little ball of light fur covered
in brown and white spikes. "It's
a hedgehog!" she exclaimed.

Look out for:

Zoe's Rescue Zoo

The Helpful Hedgehog

Amelia Cobb

Illustrated by
Sophy Williams

nosy
crow

With special thanks to Siobhan Curham

First published in the UK in 2020 by Nosy Crow Ltd
The Crow's Nest, 14 Baden Place
Crosby Row, London SE1 1YW

www.nosycrow.com

ISBN: 978 1 78800 932 4

Nosy Crow and associated logos are trademarks and/or
registered trademarks of Nosy Crow Ltd

A CIP catalogue record for this book will be available from the British Library

Printed and bound in Great Britain by Clays Ltd, Elcograf S.p.A.

Papers used by Nosy Crow are made from wood grown in sustainable forests.

1 3 5 7 9 10 8 6 4 2

Chapter One
School at the Zoo

Zoe Parker poured the milk on to her breakfast cereal, doing a little dance as she did so.

"Careful!" said Zoe's mum, Lucy, as some milk splashed on the table.

"Sorry!" Zoe said, grinning. "I'm just so excited. Today is going to be the best day ever!"

Meep, a mouse lemur and Zoe's best friend, hopped up and down on the chair next to her. Zoe passed him a bowl filled with blueberries and sliced banana. "Here's your breakfast, Meep," she said.

With a happy yelp, Meep began gobbling up the fruit. Eating was his favourite thing in the whole world. A cheery trumpeting noise outside made Zoe smile. The elephants were obviously excited about having their breakfast too.

Zoe was excited because today she wasn't going to school – her school was coming to her! Zoe's class were visiting the Rescue Zoo on a trip and her teacher, Miss Hawkins, had decided that this year they'd choose an animal to adopt. Zoe's class would learn all about the animal and visit it every half-term, and they would also create a display about it in their classroom. "I wonder which animal my class will choose," she mumbled through a mouthful of cereal.

"Well, they certainly have a *lot* to choose from," replied her mum.

Zoe looked at the clock on the wall. The class would be here soon, and Great-Uncle Horace hadn't arrived yet.

Zoe's Great-Uncle Horace was a famous explorer and animal expert. He saved animals from all over the world who were injured or endangered and brought them to live in his rescue zoo. Zoe and her mum lived at the zoo too, in a cosy cottage in the grounds. Lucy was a vet in the zoo hospital and Zoe dreamed of one day working as a zookeeper.

Great-Uncle Horace had promised he'd

give Zoe's class a talk about the zoo and about their chosen animal at a party in the café at the end of the day. He'd also said he'd join Zoe for breakfast so he could come and meet her class as they arrived.

"Do you want me to phone Uncle Horace to see what's happened?" Lucy asked.

"Yes, please," replied Zoe.

As Zoe's mum left the room to make the call, Meep leaped on to the windowsill, waving his paws excitedly.

"What is it?" asked Zoe, looking out of the window. Outside a breeze was blowing through the trees and the bright blue sky was filled with swirls of orange and gold leaves.

"It's raining leaves!" Meep chattered.

Zoe giggled. She was able to understand what the little lemur was saying because

she had a special gift – she was able to talk to animals! Nobody knew Zoe could do this, though, not even her mum or Great-Uncle Horace. It was Zoe's secret.

"It's not raining leaves, Meep," she said, stroking his silky grey fur. "It's autumn."

"I love autumn!" Meep said, but then looked a little worried. "But won't the trees get cold without their leaves?"

"No," Zoe told him. "They like it that way during the winter. And then they'll grow new ones next spring!"

Zoe's mum came back into the kitchen holding her vet's bag. "Great-Uncle Horace says he's very sorry he wasn't able to join us for breakfast. He's had to make an emergency rescue but he'll be here as soon as he can."

Zoe's heart sank. Great-Uncle Horace

rescued animals from all over the world, so there was no way to know where he might be, or when he'd be back.

"Why don't you go and wait for your class by the zoo gates when you're ready?" Lucy said, popping an apple into her vet's bag. As always, a stethoscope was poking out of the top of the bag.

"I'm ready!" cried Zoe, leaping up.

"Er, you might want to put some shoes on first," her mum said with a laugh.

Zoe looked down at her feet and giggled. She was still wearing her fluffy penguin slippers.

7

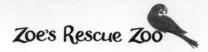

She picked up Meep and raced from the room.

As soon as she was ready, Zoe hurried out of the little cottage with Meep on her shoulder. She skipped past the lions eating their breakfast and the hippos bathing in the mud and the monkeys swinging from

their trees. She ran past the reptile house
and the nocturnal mammal house and
the petting zoo, calling a cheery "hello"
to all her animal friends as she went.
Her mum was right. There were so many
animals in the Rescue Zoo; how would
her classmates be able to choose just one
to adopt?

Finally, they reached the gates at the zoo's entrance. Meep scampered up to the top of the gate, perching on a carving of Great-Uncle Horace's hot-air balloon.

"Can I be adopted by your class, Zoe?" he chirped.

Zoe shook her head. "You've already been adopted – by me!"

Meep was the only animal in the zoo who didn't live in an enclosure. He lived with Zoe and her mum in the cottage. He even slept curled at the foot of Zoe's bed!

"They're coming! They're coming!" Meep cried as the school bus made its way down the road. Zoe's tummy fluttered with excitement as the bus came to a stop, and one by one her classmates came through the gates. At the end of the line was their teacher, Miss Hawkins.

"Today is going to be so cool!" exclaimed Zoe's friend Priti, giving her a hug.

"I can't wait to see the lions," Jack said, grinning. "And the llamas and the sloths."

"Don't forget the monkeys," added Nicola.

"My favourite are the elephants," said Elliot.

"I like the giraffes," said Grace. "Especially the baby giraffe, Jamie. He's so cute."

Zoe smiled. By the sounds of it her class wanted to adopt the entire zoo!

Meep scampered over to Zoe's friends and started dancing around their feet.

"Hello, Meep!" Priti cried, bending down to stroke him.

The last person to get off the bus was

a new boy called Toby. He was wearing
a red woolly hat and clutching the
sketchbook he took everywhere with him.
Toby had only just started at their school,
and he was really quiet.

"Hey, Toby, come and
meet Meep," Priti called.

As the others looked
at Toby, his face
blushed as red as his
hat. He shuffled over,
but instead of looking at
Meep he started flicking
through his sketchbook.

"OK, everyone, it's time to
get into groups," called Miss
Hawkins. "Then you can go
and look at the animals."

"Yay!" cheered Elliot.

"Can my group go straight to the elephants, please?"

"You can visit the animals in any order," replied Miss Hawkins, "as long as you see all of them."

Miss Hawkins divided the class into groups. Zoe was put in a group with Priti, Elliot, Jack, Toby and Grace – and Meep, of course, who had now jumped back on to her shoulder. Just as they were about to go off and explore, they heard the roar of an engine coming down the road. A Jeep screeched through the zoo gates, driven by a man with tufty white hair and a bushy white beard.

"Great-Uncle Horace!" Zoe cried. She was so pleased he'd made it in time.

"Goo! Goo!" Meep scampered over to the Jeep. Great-Uncle Horace had rescued

Meep when he was a tiny baby and, like all the animals in the zoo, Meep really loved him. He wasn't able to pronounce his name properly, so the little lemur called him Goo.

Zoe followed Meep over to the Jeep, and her class crowded round too. Great-Uncle Horace was wearing a tweed jacket and trousers and a stripy scarf. A beautiful hyacinth macaw was perched close to him. It was his beloved pet, Kiki, who went everywhere with him.

"Good morning!" bellowed Great-Uncle Horace. "I'm sorry I'm late. I had an important rescue to attend to."

Zoe's skin prickled with excitement.
She loved it when Great-Uncle Horace
brought a new animal to the zoo. What
would it be this time? She couldn't see
any animals in the Jeep – just a lot of
luggage.

"Hello, Zoe," said Great-Uncle Horace,
giving her a hug. "Hello, Meep." He bent
down to pat the little lemur on the head.
"So, would you all like to know who I've
rescued?"

"Yes, please!" the children cried.

Zoe frowned. Where could this
mysterious animal be?

Great-Uncle Horace reached into the
back seat of the Jeep and pulled out a
basket covered with a towel. "You'll have
to be very quiet, though," he said. "We
don't want to startle him."

"It must be a very small animal," said Elliot.

"I think it's a rabbit," whispered Nicola.

"Or a mouse," said Jack.

They all gathered closer as Great-Uncle Horace slowly pulled back the towel. Zoe peered inside the basket and saw a little ball of light fur covered in brown and white spikes.

"It's a hedgehog!" she exclaimed.

"An African pygmy hoglet, to be precise," replied Great-Uncle Horace with a twinkly-eyed grin.

"A *hoglet*?" asked Zoe.

"It's what you call a baby hedgehog," replied Great-Uncle Horace. "Someone set him free in the woods," Great-Uncle Horace explained. "He used to be a pet. Unfortunately once an animal like this has been kept as a pet, it has no idea how to survive in the wild."

Zoe frowned, feeling very sorry for the baby hedgehog. She wished that the hedgehog's owners had made sure he was safe instead of setting him free in the woods. He must have been scared!

"Don't worry, Zoe," said Great-Uncle Horace. "That's why I've brought him here. The zoo will be the perfect home for him."

The hedgehog looked up at Zoe with shiny black eyes. There were a few faint white whiskers on either side of his pointed nose.

"He's so sweet!" Priti exclaimed.

As the rest of the class gathered closer, the hedgehog suddenly rolled into a ball. His face completely disappeared!

"He must be feeling shy seeing so many of you," Great-Uncle Horace said. "Never mind. I'll go and get him settled into his new home at the nocturnal mammal house."

"Ooh, can I come too?" cried Zoe. She loved helping the new animals get settled into the zoo, especially because she was able to talk to them. It helped them feel welcome and happy.

"I don't see why not," replied Great-Uncle Horace. "As long as it's OK with Miss Hawkins."

"I promise I won't be long," Zoe told Miss Hawkins earnestly. "I'll catch up with my group."

Miss Hawkins nodded. "Fine with me!"

"Thank you!" As Zoe set off with Great-Uncle Horace and Meep, she turned to see which way her group were going. Priti, Elliot, Jack and Grace were all chatting excitedly together as they headed towards the

elephant enclosure – but the new boy,
Toby, was trailing far behind them.

Zoe sighed. Poor Toby looked really sad.
But the sight of the animals at the Rescue
Zoo would cheer him up for sure!

At least, Zoe hoped so.

Chapter Two

The Topsy-Turvy House

The nocturnal mammal house was in a
quiet part of the zoo, surrounded by tall
oak trees. The ground outside was covered
with orange, yellow and brown leaves.
Zoe loved the crunching sound they
made under her feet.

As she followed Great-Uncle Horace
inside, she had to squint to see the

enclosures around her. It was so dark in the nocturnal house! It had to be dim because the animals who lived there liked to be awake at night and asleep during the day. Zoe called the nocturnal house the "topsy-turvy house" because at night the keepers turned all the lights on so that it seemed like daytime, and the nocturnal animals all went to sleep. But right now, during the day, they pretended it was night so that the animals would be awake for people to see.

As her eyes adjusted, Zoe saw the bats fluttering around in the blue light of their enclosure. In the enclosure opposite, a friendly chinchilla called Suki was climbing on a branch. She gave a loud squeak of welcome as soon as she saw Zoe and Great-Uncle Horace.

Alice, the keeper in charge of the nocturnal mammal house, came hurrying over. "Hello, Zoe. Hello, Mr Higgins. Do you have a new arrival for me?"

"We certainly do," said Great-Uncle Horace.

"It's a hedgehog – I mean, a hoglet," said Zoe. "Great-Uncle Horace had to rescue him because he wasn't safe in the wild."

Alice smiled. "Is that so? Well, he'll be very safe here. There's an enclosure free at the end of the row. I'll prepare him some food and we can get him all set up."

"What do hedgehogs eat?" asked Zoe.

"Fruits and vegetables," replied Alice.

At the mention of food Meep did a little dance at Zoe's feet.

"And mealworms, and a special feed

made for insectivores," continued Alice.

"Yuck!" chirped Meep.

Zoe couldn't answer Meep, as no one knew she could understand him. She swallowed her smile and asked, "What's an insectivore?"

"An animal that eats insects and worms," explained Alice.

"Double yuck!" Meep chattered, pulling a face. Zoe had to bite her lip to keep from giggling.

"I'll help Alice get the food," said Great-Uncle Horace, handing Zoe the basket. "Can you show this little fellow to his new home?"

"Of course," replied Zoe.

She made her way to the empty enclosure at the end of the row, carrying the basket very carefully. She didn't

want to startle the little hedgehog again.
Placing the basket on the ground, she
removed the towel from the top. The
hoglet slowly uncurled himself and stared
up at her.

"Don't be afraid," Zoe whispered. "My
name's Zoe, and you're at my Great-
Uncle Horace's Rescue Zoo. Lots of
animals live here, so you'll be able to
make loads of new friends."

"I'll be your friend!" Mcep chattered, jumping up and down so he could see inside the basket.

"That's Meep," Zoe said. "What's your name?"

The hedgehog made a snuffling sound.

"Hugo!" Zoe exclaimed. "What a lovely name."

The hedgehog purred.

"Do you want to see your new home?"

Zoe put her hand in the basket and laid it out flat. The hedgehog shuffled over and sniffed at her fingers, then crawled on to her palm. Zoe lifted Hugo out of the basket and showed him the enclosure. There was soil on the bottom, and it was filled with lots of pretty plants to hide in and sturdy branches to climb. That was another topsy-turvy thing about the nocturnal mammal house – it looked just like the outside, inside!

Hugo squeaked excitedly.

"Yes, you'll be able to root and burrow here," replied Zoe.

"What does root and burrow mean?" asked Meep.

"It's when animals make a home for themselves underground."

"Can *we* make a home underground?" chirped Meep.

Zoe laughed. "I'm not sure Great-Uncle Horace would want us digging up his zoo." She carefully placed Hugo into his enclosure and the little hedgehog looked around, sniffing at some of the rocks and leaves. Then he came back over to Zoe and squeaked.

"What did he say?" asked Meep.

"He said that the old lady who used to be his owner had to move house, and she wasn't allowed to take pets with her – apart from her special assistance dog who helps her," explained Zoe. "That's why she set Hugo free in the woods."

Hugo snuffled. He wished he was helpful enough to have been able to go with his old owner.

"Oh, don't be sad, Hugo. Assistance dogs are specially trained. I'm sure hedgehogs can be very helpful too."

"Am I helpful?" chattered Meep.

"Yes! You're always helpful at letting me know when it's time to eat!" replied Zoe with a giggle.

Hugo grunted.

"The woods must have been scary," replied Zoe. "I'm glad you feel a lot safer now."

Just then Alice and Great-Uncle Horace returned.

"I hope our hoglet is ready for his breakfast!" Great-Uncle Horace announced.

Hugo gave a contented purr as Alice placed a dish of berries into the enclosure.

"My, he does seem happy," said Great-

Uncle Horace. "Great work, Zoe."

Zoe beamed with pride. "His name's Hugo," she told him.

"Very good," replied Great-Uncle Horace. "You always come up with the most excellent names."

Zoe grinned at Hugo. She hadn't come up with that name – Hugo had told her himself!

"Right, I need to visit some of the other animals," said Great-Uncle Horace. "I'll see you later at the party in the café."

"OK." As Great-Uncle Horace strode off towards the exit, Zoe scooped up Meep and leaned into the enclosure. "I need to go now, Hugo, but I'll be back soon, I promise."

Hugo made a whimpering sound and scuttled over to the front of the enclosure.

"I won't be gone for long," said Zoe.
But Hugo continued to whimper. "I don't
think he wants to be left on his own," Zoe
said to Alice. "Would it be OK if I take
him with me?"

"Sure," replied
Alice. "If that
will make him
feel better, go
ahead!"

"Cool!"
Zoe placed
her hand on
the ground of
the enclosure
and Hugo
quickly shuffled
on, purring
happily.

32

She'd make sure Hugo felt safe — that was the most important way that Zoe and Meep could help the animals at the Rescue Zoo. Now it was time to go and find her friends.

Chapter Three
A Prickly Ball

Carefully placing Hugo on one shoulder and Meep on the other, Zoe set off through the zoo.

"Over there's the snake house," she said to Hugo, pointing to the building next door to the nocturnal house.

Hugo grunted a question in her ear.

"Snakes are reptiles," replied Zoe.

"They're long and thin and have scaly skin."

"And they sound like thisssssssss," said Meep, giving a long hiss.

Hugo started to giggle.

"And here's the meerkat enclosure," Zoe continued. "Meerkats love to burrow too. Would you like to see them?"

Hugo grunted that he would.

Zoe went over to the meerkat enclosure and felt for the silver paw-print charm on her necklace. It had been a gift from Great-Uncle Horace – the charm opened the gates to all the enclosures in the zoo! Zoe held the charm next to a pad on the gate. It swung open.

Meep scampered down from her shoulder and over to a log where Max the meerkat was standing with his tummy facing the sun. Zoe giggled as Meep stood as tall as he could, copying the meerkat.

"Hello, Max! I want you to meet Hugo the hedgehog; he's new to the zoo." Zoe took Hugo down from her shoulder.

Max gave a cheery yelp.

Hugo looked at Zoe and squeaked.

"He's asking if he can see you burrow," said Zoe.

The little meerkat hopped off the log and started digging a hole in the sandy ground with his back feet.

"Hey!" Meep cried as a cloud of sand covered him. "First it was raining leaves, now it's raining sand." The lemur grumbled and hopped back up on to Zoe's shoulder.

Hugo giggled.

"OK, we'd better catch up with my

group," said Zoe. "See you later, Max."

Max yelped and carried on digging.

As Zoe put Hugo back on her shoulder, the little hedgehog squeaked in her ear.

"Yes, meerkats are very good at burrowing," she replied.

"A bit too good!" Meep huffed in her other ear.

The next enclosure they came to belonged to the pandas. Half of Zoe's class were gathered outside it, watching as the panda twins Chi-Chi and Mei-Mei snacked on bamboo canes.

"These are the panda bears," Zoe whispered to Hugo. "They've come all the way from a country called China."

Hugo gave a frightened snuffle.

"I know they're very big, but they won't hurt you," said Zoe. "All the animals here are really friendly."

Hugo peeked at the panda twins again and then made a friendly clicking noise.

Zoe carried on along the winding footpath through the zoo. The air was filled with the excited chatter of her classmates.

Hugo grunted a question in her ear.

"Yes, there are always lots of children at the zoo, but today there's even more – my class are visiting!" Zoe explained. "They've come to find an animal to adopt for the year. We'll learn about the animal in class and come to visit it every term."

Hugo snuffled excitedly.

"Yes, it'd be lovely if they chose you," agreed Zoe.

Then Hugo sighed and gave a sad little snort.

"Just because other animals are bigger than you, it doesn't make them more exciting," said Zoe.

"Small animals can be exciting too," Meep chirped. He performed a little backflip to prove his point.

"Yes, they can," agreed Zoe. "And anyway, even if my class doesn't adopt you, lots of really nice people visit the zoo every day, so you'll still have plenty of friends."

Hugo sniffed, saying that he wasn't so sure.

Zoe saw her group over by the lion

enclosure. "Come on, let's go and see Leonard and Rory. Leonard is a very old lion and Rory is a lion cub," she explained.

Hugo grunted.

"Yes, lions are very brave and cool," Zoe agreed before going over to join her friends. "But you're just as cool!"

"Hey, Zoe," said Grace. "Did you get the baby hedgehog settled into his new home?"

Zoe nodded.

"Can we go and see him next?" asked Jack. "The nocturnal mammal house is amazing. It's like being in the middle of the night – in the middle of the day!"

"You can see him right now," replied Zoe. She lifted up her hair so her classmates could see the little hedgehog nestled on her shoulder.

"Aw, he looks so cosy," said Priti.

Zoe noticed Toby sitting on the ground next to the enclosure, drawing a picture of Rory in his sketch pad.

"Wow, that's a really great picture, Toby," she said. "It looks like Rory's just about to jump off the page!"

Toby looked embarrassed and said, "Thanks." But he gave a little smile when he saw Hugo.

Just then Mr Pinch, the zoo manager, came stomping up the path towards them, holding a broom.

"Uh-oh," Zoe muttered. Mr Pinch had a habit of being grumpy about just about everything.

"I hate autumn," he grumbled, as he started sweeping up a pile of leaves. "It's

just so messy with all these leaves all over the place. Why can't they stay where they belong, on the trees? And you children aren't making it any better," he added, looking straight at Zoe. "How am I supposed to sweep away the leaves with you cluttering up the footpaths?"

Zoe shook her head at him.

The zoo needed people to visit!
The animals liked people visiting!
Mr Pinch was just cross that it got in
the way of his tidying.

"Don't worry," Zoe whispered to Toby.
"He's always grumpy."

Toby gave a relieved smile and carried
on drawing.

Zoe went over to join Jack and
Elliot, who were sitting on a wall
by the enclosure. Meep hopped
on to the wall beside them and Zoe
carefully placed Hugo on her lap.

"The elephants were so cool," said
Elliot. "They've definitely got my vote."

"But what about the lions?" asked Jack.
"They're so strong."

"We haven't seen the penguins yet," said Priti, coming over to join them.

"Or the zebras," said Grace.

As her group started arguing about which animal they each wanted to adopt, Zoe sighed. They were never going to agree!

All of a sudden Mr Pinch gave a yell. "Ow! I've been attacked by some prickly leaves!"

Zoe looked down at her lap … and found that it was empty! "Where's Hugo?" she said. She hopped down from the wall and looked over at Mr Pinch. "Uh-oh," she said when she saw a ball of leaves in his hand. A very spiky ball of leaves! "I'm so sorry, Mr Pinch. That's Hugo, the baby hedgehog. Great-Uncle Horace just rescued him."

"Then what, may I ask, is he doing hiding in some leaves?" spluttered Mr Pinch.

"I was just showing him around the zoo, to help him get settled in."

"How many times do I have to tell you, you can't let animals run wild," Mr Pinch scolded her.

"I'm sorry, it won't happen again," said Zoe as she carefully took Hugo from him. His spikes were now covered in orange and brown leaves.

"It had better not!" said Mr Pinch crossly, picking up his broom and sweeping away.

"I think we should go and see some other animals," Zoe whispered to her friends.

"Good idea," Grace agreed.

"Let's go to the petting zoo," said Priti. "I want to see the goats."

As Zoe's friends started making their way to the petting zoo, Zoe hung back so she could talk to Hugo without them hearing.

"You can't just run off like that," she told him as she removed the leaves from his spikes. "You might get lost!"

Hugo gave a sad little snuffle.

"You were trying to help Mr Pinch clear up the leaves?" exclaimed Zoe. "Oh, Hugo, that's really nice of you."

Hugo gave another sad snuffle.

"Don't be embarrassed – you don't look silly," said Zoe, removing the final leaf. "It was a really kind thing to do, even if it didn't quite work out." She placed the little hedgehog back on her shoulder. "Come on, let's find you some more friends."

There had to be someone in the zoo that could make Hugo feel at home!

Chapter Four
Missing Hedgehog!

The petting zoo was in the middle of the zoo behind the café and gift shop. Another group of Zoe's classmates were there when she arrived, gathered around the rabbit hutches.

Tony, the keeper in charge of the petting zoo, was sweeping out the pigsties. "Hello, Zoe," he called. "Would you and your friends like to feed the animals their lunch?"

A cheer rang out from Zoe's classmates.

"Oh yes, please!" exclaimed Zoe. She put Hugo down on the floor next to the goat enclosure and Meep hopped down from her other shoulder. "Now don't go anywhere," she whispered to the little hedgehog. "I'm just going to get some food for the goats. I'll be straight back."

Hugo purred happily and snuggled against the fence.

Zoe placed her school bag on the floor next to Hugo then went over to the shed where the food was kept. As she opened the door, Meep scampered inside.

"Is it lunchtime for me too?" he chattered.

"Not yet," Zoe told him.

Meep sighed.

Zoe took the container of goat feed from the shelf and poured some into a bucket. Then she took the bucket back outside. Thankfully Hugo was exactly where she'd left him. A goat called Greta had come over to the fence and was sniffing the little hedgehog inquisitively.

"This is Greta," said Zoe, putting the goat feed on the ground next to Hugo. "And Greta, this is Hugo — he's just arrived at the Rescue Zoo." Zoe leaned over the fence and patted Greta on the head. The little goat gave Hugo a welcoming bleat, and one by one the other goats trotted over to say hello. "I'm just going to get some food for the rabbits, then my classmates and I will give you your lunch," Zoe added. She went back into the shed and filled another bucket with some chopped carrot and watercress.

"I'm so hungry!" Meep wailed, making his ears flop and his tail droop.

"Oh, OK then, have this." Zoe said with a smile, and handed him a piece of carrot.

The little lemur did a happy dance and started nibbling at the carrot, making Zoe giggle. But as she came out of the shed, her smile faded. Hugo was still by the goat enclosure, but now he was butting his head against the food bucket.

"What's Hugo doing?" Meep chattered.

"I'm not sure. Let's go and see."

But as Zoe and Meep hurried over, Hugo gave the bucket an extra big nudge and it toppled over, spilling the food under the fence.

The goats snorted excitedly and started

gobbling up their lunch.

"Oh no!" cried Priti. "The goats are eating already. Now we won't be able to feed them."

Zoe's classmates all looked really disappointed. All except Toby, who was

looking at Hugo and grinning. The
hedgehog did look funny, with his spikes
covered in grain from the goat feed.

"I was really looking forward to feeding
the goats," said Grace, sticking her bottom
lip out.

"Don't worry, you can still feed the rabbits," said Zoe, hurrying over and handing her the bucket. Her classmates gathered round and took handfuls of feed to give to the rabbits. Even Toby joined in, taking a carrot to feed them.

"Feed *me*! Feed *me*!" Meep chattered, scampering around the children's feet. Zoe was very glad she was the only one who could understand him. If her whole class fed Meep, there'd be nothing left for the rabbits!

"Come on, Meep," she said, scooping him up into her arms. "Let's go and check on Hugo. I'm going to have to clean his spikes all over again!"

"He was so funny when he knocked the bucket over," said Jack, leaning over the fence to give one of the rabbits some carrot and watercress.

"I know," giggled Grace.

"And he looks even funnier covered in food," said Elliot.

Zoe chuckled, but when she turned round she could see no sign of Hugo. "Oh no, where's he gone now?"

Zoe and Meep hurried over to the goat enclosure, but the little hedgehog was nowhere to be seen.

"Hugo's missing!" she cried.

Her friends came hurrying over.

"Maybe he's in the shed," said Jack.

Zoe ran and checked but the shed was empty.

"What about that hay?" Priti suggested, pointing to a bale on the other side of the enclosure.

"Oh yes, he might have burrowed inside

it," replied Zoe. She searched through the hay, but there was still no sign of Hugo. Zoe went back to her friends. "I can't believe he's disappeared," she said, feeling worried.

Just then Miss Hawkins arrived. "OK, everybody, it's time for lunch!" she called.

As her classmates went off to the café, Zoe had one final look for Hugo, but he was still nowhere to be seen.

"How am I going to tell Great-Uncle Horace that I've lost him?" she said to Meep.

Meep's ears flopped and his tail drooped. This time Zoe knew he wasn't pretending. The little lemur looked just as sad as she felt.

"Well," she said, "we can't search the whole zoo by ourselves on an empty stomach, so let's eat something and then get the rest of the class to help us look for Hugo." Zoe opened her school bag to get out her money for lunch. "Ow!" she cried, quickly pulling her hand back out.

"What is it?" Meep chattered.

"There's something spiky in my bag." Zoe's eyes lit up. She opened the backpack wide and, sure enough, there was Hugo, curled up in a ball.

"Hugo, what are you doing in there?" exclaimed Zoe.

The little hedgehog uncurled just enough to show the tip of his nose and gave a sad little grunt.

"Why are you hiding?" asked Zoe.

Hugo uncurled a little more and his shiny black eyes appeared. He grunted again.

"Why are you embarrassed?" Zoe put her hand in the bag, palm facing upwards. Hugo climbed on and Zoe placed him on her lap.

Hugo looked up at her and whimpered.

"No one's cross with you!" exclaimed Zoe.

"What's going on?" Meep asked, hopping on to Zoe's shoulder.

"He thinks my classmates are angry with him for knocking over the goat feed. He thinks they won't want to adopt him." Zoe wished Hugo didn't become so prickly when he was upset. She really wanted to give him a hug! "They know it was an accident, Hugo."

Hugo gave another sad little grunt.

"You knocked it over on purpose?" said Zoe. "But why?"

"Maybe he was hungry," said Meep.

The little hedgehog shook his head and snuffled. Zoe couldn't help smiling as Hugo explained that he wanted to help feed the goats.

"Well, in that case, you definitely aren't in trouble," said Zoe. "You were just trying to be helpful." She picked the pieces of goat feed from Hugo's spikes. "Let's go and have some lunch. Then I'll show you some more of the zoo."

As Zoe set off for the café with Hugo and Meep, she couldn't help wondering what else might happen today. Life certainly wasn't boring with Hugo around!

Chapter Five
Interesting Hedgehog Facts

After lunch, Zoe's group decided to go and see the sea otters.

"You're going to love the otters," Zoe whispered to Hugo as she made her way along the footpath with Meep dancing at her feet. "They're really friendly, and they're great swimmers."

The otters lived in a saltwater pool at

the far end of the zoo. Clusters of rocks lined the lake for the otters to sit on when they weren't in the water. When Zoe and her friends got there, Sasha the sea otter was floating on her back.

Seeing Zoe at the edge of the enclosure, Sasha came swimming over. Thankfully Zoe's classmates went over to see some baby sea otters snuggled together on one of the rocks, so she was able to talk to Sasha.

"Hi there! I'd like to introduce you to Hugo," she said, showing the little hedgehog to the sea otter. "He's new!"

Sasha gave Hugo a welcoming whistle and Hugo squeaked hello. When they were done, Sasha splashed back off into the middle of the pool to fish for her breakfast.

As Zoe walked round the edge of the enclosure, she noticed Toby sitting on his own next to the glass wall. He still looked really sad.

"Oh, poor Toby, he's all on his own," she said.

Quick as a flash, Meep leaped down from her shoulder and scampered over to Toby, bounding on to his lap.

Toby yelped in surprise and dropped his sketch pad.

Zoe hurried over and sat down next to him as Meep moved a few steps away. "Sorry about that," she said with a smile. "Meep was just trying to be friendly, but sometimes he can be a little bouncy!" She took Hugo down from her shoulder and placed him on the ground.

"That's OK," said Toby, staring at the

little hedgehog.

"Meep's a mouse lemur," said Zoe. "My
Great-Uncle Horace rescued him when
he was a baby, and he's been my best
friend ever since." Talking about her best
friend made Zoe feel bad for Toby. It
was hard enough being the new kid at
school, but he was so shy that he hadn't

really made friends with anyone in their class yet. It must be very lonely to be far away from your old school and not to have anyone to talk to at your new one!

Toby was still looking at Hugo, who had shuffled over to him and was making friendly squeaks.

"Ah, Hugo's saying hello to you,"

said Zoe. "I think he really likes you," she added.

Toby gave her a little smile. "Really?"

"Yes. Look, now he's nuzzling you. Animals only do that if they really like you."

Toby's smile grew a bit bigger. "I really like him too. Hedgehogs are so cool."

"I know," agreed Zoe. "We've never had one at the zoo before. I'm really excited to learn all about him."

Toby nodded. "I've never seen a real one up close before. Did you know that hedgehogs have a really good sense of smell?"

Zoe shook her head.

"Yes, it helps them to find food."

Hugo grunted.

"And did you know that baby

hedgehogs lose their spikes the same way humans lose their baby teeth?"

"Really?" Zoe's eyes grew wider. She loved learning new things about animals – it was cool that Toby knew so much and wasn't too shy to tell her about it!

Hugo grunted loudly, agreeing with Toby.

"Yes, and when they lose their spikes it feels really itchy. So they can get a bit grumpy," said Toby.

Hugo grunted even louder.

"It sounds like he's agreeing with you," said Zoe, trying not to laugh. Because she could understand Hugo she knew he was *definitely* agreeing with Toby! "How do you know so much about hedgehogs?" she asked.

"I love animals," Toby told her. "I used

to read about them a lot at the library in my old school." Then he picked up his sketch pad. "Would it be OK if I drew a picture of him?"

"Of course." Zoe watched as Toby took a pencil from his school bag and started drawing. It was so nice to see him happy. She tried to think of something else that might make him smile.

"There are going to be some really cool goody bags at the party. They've got animal stickers in them, and strawberry- and lemon-flavoured sweets."

"Oh, a party?" Toby said, frowning. "I don't know. I don't really like strawberries either."

"Oh." Zoe's heart sank. Just when she thought Toby was cheering up, he seemed to feel sad again. Zoe thought that maybe he was worried about being around all the other children at the party, and being too shy to talk to anyone.

Just then Zoe's mum appeared. "Hi, Zoe. Can you and Meep come and help me set up for the party?"

"Sure." Zoe stood up. "I'm going to have to take Hugo with me," she said to Toby, carefully picking up the hedgehog. "But you can carry on drawing him at the party if you like."

"OK," said Toby, but his smile had completely faded. He looked just as sad as

69

before, and he wasn't the only one. Hugo gave a little whimper as Zoe placed him back on her shoulder.

Oh dear, Zoe thought. She hated the idea of anyone feeling upset. What could she do to cheer Hugo and Toby up?

Chapter Six
A Giant BANG!

When Zoe arrived at the café with her mum, Meep and Hugo, there was a sign on the door saying CLOSED FOR PRIVATE PARTY. The only person in the café was Sally, the café manager.

"Hi there!" she called from behind the counter. "Come and have a look at the cupcakes I've made for your class."

Keeping a tight hold of Meep, who couldn't be trusted when it came to food, Zoe made her way behind the counter.

"Wow, they look delicious!" she exclaimed. The cupcakes were decorated with thick white frosting and topped with miniature animals made from fondant.

Meep waved his paws up and down in excitement as he spotted a cake with a little mouse lemur on top.

"Oh, who's this?" Sally asked, pointing to Hugo.

"This is Hugo." Zoe carefully took the hedgehog down from her shoulder. "He arrived at the zoo today."

"What a shame he didn't get here sooner! I would have made a hedgehog cupcake too. Although…" Sally started to smile. "Will you two be OK for a while? I just need to do something in the kitchen."

"Of course," Zoe's mum, Lucy, replied. "We'll get on with decorating and laying the tables."

Once they had covered the tables with animal-themed tablecloths, Lucy took some party bags and a big jar of sweets from a box.

"Could you put the sweets in the bags while I go and get the balloons from the cottage?" she asked Zoe.

"Of course," agreed Zoe. This would give her the chance to make sure Toby didn't get any strawberry sweets in his bag. Hopefully that would make him feel better! She tipped the sweets on to the table and Hugo grunted loudly.

"You want to help me?" Zoe frowned. She wasn't really sure how Hugo would be able to help, but then she remembered what Toby had said about a hedgehog's sense of smell. "Can you sniff out all the strawberry sweets and put them into a pile?" she asked.

Hugo grunted excitedly and started sniffing the sweets.

"Can I help eat the sweets?" Meep chattered, bouncing up and down on a chair next to Zoe.

"No!" exclaimed Zoe. She looked around the café for something else Meep could do. "I know, you can help with the decorations." She picked up a string of animal bunting and handed it to Meep. "Can you hang this along the shelf?"

Meep scampered off with the bunting, chattering excitedly.

The three of them continued sniffing and sorting and decorating for a few minutes, until Lucy returned with the balloons and a very flustered-looking Mr Pinch.

"As if I haven't got enough to do," he

grumbled. "Since when has blowing up balloons been part of managing a zoo?"

"But you're just so good at getting things done, Mr Pinch," Lucy said, winking at Zoe. "With your help, we'll get this place ready for the party in no time."

"Well, yes, that's very true," Mr Pinch said with a nod. "I'm definitely the best at organising in this zoo."

Zoe focused on finishing the last of the party bags, trying not to giggle. She packed a bag especially for Toby, avoiding the pile of strawberry sweets Hugo had made on the table.

"Thank you," she whispered to the little hedgehog. "You were very helpful." She looked around for Meep, who was perched on the shelf where he'd hung the bunting. Zoe guessed he didn't want to come down while Mr Pinch was in the café. Mr Pinch was always really grumpy with the little lemur.

Zoe joined her mum and Mr Pinch in blowing up balloons and placing them on the table. "The café looks so cool," she said. "This is going to be a fantastic party."

"Humph!" said Mr Pinch as he finished blowing up a balloon.

Suddenly there was a giant BANG! Zoe and Lucy jumped.

"Aaaargh!" yelled Mr Pinch, letting go of the balloon he was about to tie up, causing it to shoot around the room like a rocket. "What was that?"

Zoe looked down at the table. Hugo was sitting in the middle of the balloons, looking very embarrassed. The remains of a burst purple balloon was stuck to his spikes.

"What is that animal doing there?" Mr Pinch yelled.

Hugo looked up at Zoe and squeaked.

"I think he was just trying to help with the balloons," said Zoe.

"Trying to help?" Mr Pinch's face went as purple as the balloon that had burst. "Animals are meant to be on display, not running loose all over the zoo, prickling things and causing a mess."

"I'm sorry, Mr Pinch," Zoe apologised. "It was only an accident."

"Well, I've had quite enough hedgehog accidents for one day," huffed Mr Pinch. "I'm off to get on with my proper work."

Zoe watched as he stomped out of the café.

"Don't worry, love," said Lucy, giving Zoe a hug. "You know what Mr Pinch is like. He's always grumbling about something."

Zoe nodded. *She* knew what Mr Pinch was like, but Hugo didn't. She looked back at the hedgehog. He was curled into a tight ball with his face completely hidden.

"Please don't worry," Zoe whispered as Lucy went to see Sally in the kitchen.

"Please come back out." But it was no good. Hugo stayed in a tight little ball with all his spikes fully extended.

Zoe felt terrible. The poor little hedgehog had only been trying to be useful. Now Zoe would never be able to help Hugo settle in and feel welcome at the zoo!

Chapter Seven
Where's Toby?

Zoe heard the sound of chatter outside.
"My class are here!" she cried. Then she
carefully scooped Hugo up and put him
in her jacket pocket. "Come on, Meep."
The little mouse lemur scampered down
from the shelf and on to her shoulder.

Zoe's classmates were gathered on
the grass in front of the café. They were

arguing so loudly about which animal to adopt, Zoe could hardly hear herself think.

"I think we should adopt a llama," said a boy called Danny. "They're really good at herding and they've come all the way from South America."

"But what about the koalas?" replied a girl called Jessica. "They've come all the way from Australia."

"So have the kangaroos," said Jack. "*And* they can jump really high."

Meep hopped down from Zoe's shoulder and started jumping up and down. "Look, see?" he chattered. "I can jump too."

Zoe giggled and picked him up. "I told you, you're not up for adoption," she whispered.

"I still think the elephants are the best,"

said Elliott.

Zoe spotted Toby standing behind him, staring at the floor. His hat was pulled down so far she could hardly see his face.

"All right, quiet down, everyone," called Miss Hawkins. "You'll each get a chance to have your say about the animal you'd like to adopt once we get inside the café. Every student will take a turn."

Toby pulled his hat down even further. He looked really nervous. Zoe was about to go over to see if he was all right when her mum called her over.

"Would you show everyone where to go please, Zoe?" she asked.

Zoe looked to her mum and then to Toby. She'd make sure to talk to him later. She opened the café door and her classmates hurried in, finally stopping

their arguing as they all admired the
decorations.

"Wow, it looks amazing!" exclaimed
Grace. "I love the animal bunting."

Meep chattered proudly.

"And look at the goody bags – they've
got animals on them too," said Priti.

"I hope I get one with an elephant on
it," said Elliot.

Zoe looked around for Toby to give him
his special goody bag, but she couldn't see
him.

"Has anyone seen Toby?" she called.

"He was here a minute ago," said Elliot,
looking around.

Miss Hawkins came hurrying over.
"What's the matter, Zoe?"

"It's Toby, he's missing!" replied Zoe.

"Toby!" called Miss Hawkins, as the rest

of the class fell silent. "Toby, where
are you?"

Zoe searched the café but
there was no sign of him. "It's
so strange. I saw him outside
just now. Maybe he's still out
there." Zoe ran to the door
and looked. The sun was
setting, and the old-
fashioned street lights
had come on. The
grass and the footpath
were covered in a pretty
golden glow. But there
was no sign of Toby.

"He's gone," said Zoe,
coming back into the café.
Her tummy fluttered with nerves.
Where could he be?

"OK, everyone, I want you to get back into your groups. Split up and look for him," said Miss Hawkins. "He can't have gone far."

Zoe followed her group to the elephant enclosure. All around the zoo she could hear her friends calling, "Toby!"

While the rest of her group checked behind the elephant keeper's shed, Zoe went over to the enclosure, where Bertie the baby elephant was waving his trunk.

"Hello, Bertie," Zoe whispered.

Bertie lifted his trunk and trumpeted.

"We're looking for someone wearing a red hat," replied Zoe. "Have you seen him?"

Bertie trumpeted again.

"You saw someone with a red hat over by the monkeys?"

Bertie nodded.

"That's great, thank you!" Zoe said and hurried back to her friends.

"He's not here," Priti said sadly.

"Don't worry." Zoe patted her friend's arm. "Let's try the monkeys."

As they ran along the path to the monkey enclosure, Zoe's skin tingled with relief. Thanks to Bertie, they'd soon find Toby.

But when they got there he was still nowhere to be seen. Mickey, a spider

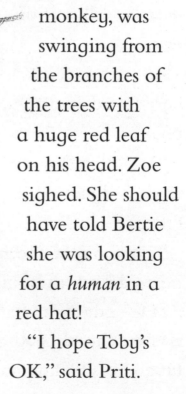

monkey, was swinging from the branches of the trees with a huge red leaf on his head. Zoe sighed. She should have told Bertie she was looking for a *human* in a red hat!

"I hope Toby's OK," said Priti.

"He did look really nervous when we were waiting outside the café," said Zoe.

"Especially when Miss Hawkins said we'd all take it in turns to talk about the animal we want to adopt," said Grace.

"Maybe he ran away because he didn't want to talk in front of everyone," said Priti.

Zoe felt so silly. Of course, Toby would hate the idea of that! No wonder he'd run off.

"Maybe he's gone back to see the lions," suggested Jack. "I think he really liked them."

"Let's go and check," said Elliot.

As they set off along the winding path, Zoe heard a squeak from her jacket pocket. She stopped and carefully took Hugo out. "What is it?" she whispered.

The little hedgehog squeaked again.

"What did he say?" asked Meep, scampering around Zoe's feet.

"Hugo said that when he's scared he likes to go somewhere quiet and dark." Zoe looked back at Hugo. "Do you think Toby might be the same?"

Hugo nodded and squeaked.

Zoe grinned at Meep. "Come on! I think I know where he is!"

Chapter Eight
Hugo to the Rescue

Zoe and Meep raced into the nocturnal mammal house, the quietest and darkest place in the zoo. They looked around, but apart from an old man looking at Suki the chinchilla, there was no one else in sight.

Zoe felt disappointed. She had been so sure Toby would be there!

Hugo grunted from her pocket.

"Good idea!" replied Zoe.

"What did he say?" Meep asked.

"Hugo said that when he's scared, he likes to curl up, and maybe Toby feels the same way. He wants us to look over by his enclosure." They headed to the far end of the nocturnal house. And, just as Hugo had suggested, Toby was sitting by the hedgehog's enclosure. His sketch pad was on the floor beside him and his knees were pulled up to his chest.

"Hello," said Zoe.

Toby glanced up at her. "Hello," he mumbled.

Zoe felt Hugo moving around in her pocket, so she took him out and sat down beside Toby. Meep sat on the other side of him.

"Everyone's looking for you," said Zoe. "Do you want to come back to the café?"

Toby shook his head.

Hugo grunted and shuffled across Zoe's lap towards Toby.

"I think he wants to sit on your lap," said Zoe.

Toby's eyes lit up. "Really?"

"Yes, really!" Carefully, Zoe passed the hedgehog to him.

As soon as he was on Toby's lap, Hugo started purring.

"That means he's happy," Zoe explained.

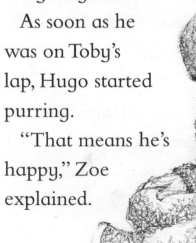

Toby gave a little smile. "I've been working on the picture of him. Do you want to see?"

"Yes, please!"

Toby picked up his sketch pad and opened it. In the dim light Zoe could just make out a drawing of Hugo sitting on one of the logs in his enclosure.

"Wow, that's great!" exclaimed Zoe warmly. "You're so good at drawing."

Hugo grunted in agreement.

Toby's face flushed, and he smiled a little. "Thank you."

At the other end of the nocturnal house the door burst open and Zoe's group came running in.

"There she is," cried Priti. "And, look, she's found Toby!"

Zoe's friends hurried over.

"Are you OK?" asked Elliot.

Toby nodded, staring down shyly at the floor.

"He's drawn a really cool picture of Hugo," said Zoe. "Do you want to see?"

"Yes please," her friends exclaimed, and they all gathered round.

"Cool!" said Grace.

"It looks just like him," Jack added.

"Great job!" Elliot praised him.

Toby beamed with pride and Hugo nuzzled him affectionately.

"Aw, look, Hugo really likes you," said Grace.

Toby's smile grew even bigger.

"Do you want to go back to the party?" asked Elliot.

"The café looks amazing," said Priti. "It's full of animal decorations."

"And we've all got party bags," said Jack.

"You see?" Zoe whispered to Toby. "Everyone really wants you there. The class isn't complete without you!" Hugo squeaked in agreement.

Toby looked up at all the friendly faces around him and smiled. "OK," he agreed.

"I'll come." He passed Hugo back to Zoe carefully and stood up, looking content.

As Zoe followed her friends out of the nocturnal house, she held Hugo close. "Thanks so much for helping to find Toby," she whispered.

Hugo purred happily. He was a helpful hedgehog after all!

Chapter Nine
Adopted Animal!

Once Zoe's class were all back in the café
and sitting at their tables, Great-Uncle
Horace got up and stood in front of the
counter.

"Welcome, everyone!" he boomed.
"Thank you so much for visiting the
Rescue Zoo. I hope you've all had a
wonderful time."

The class cheered in agreement.

"Excellent!" Great-Uncle Horace said with a grin. "Now it's time for you to choose an animal to adopt. This will be a very hard choice, as all animals are special in different ways. Who would like to talk first about the animal they'd like the class to adopt?"

A girl called Jessica put her hand up. "I'd like us to adopt a koala because they have pouches."

"So do kangaroos!" called Jack.

"I'd like us to adopt a giraffe because they have such long necks," said a boy called Ryan. "I wish I had a neck that long!"

"Yes, but think of the trouble you'd have finding a scarf to fit," said Great-Uncle Horace.

Zoe's classmates giggled.

"Would anyone else like to talk about the animal they like the best?" asked Great-Uncle Horace.

Toby shifted in his seat next to Zoe. Then, to her surprise, he stood up.

"I really like hedgehogs," he murmured.

"Did you say hedgehogs?" asked Great-Uncle Horace.

Toby nodded.

"Excellent. And why is that?"

"Because hedgehogs are so interesting." Toby looked down at Hugo, who was sitting in front of him on the table.

"Go on, you can pick him up!" Zoe whispered to Toby. "Just put your hand out flat!"

Toby looked nervous but nodded, and moved his hand next to Hugo for him to

climb on. Hugo looked a little nervous
too, but finally stepped on to Toby's hand.

Toby beamed with happiness, and lifted
Hugo for the whole class to see. Everyone
loved it!

"They have a really great sense of
smell," said Toby, pointing to Hugo's
nose. "It helps them find food and detect
danger."

At the mention of food Meep, who was sitting on Zoe's lap, waved his paws excitedly. "Maybe Hugo can help me find some treats!" he chattered.

"Another interesting fact about hedgehogs is that they each have between five thousand and seven thousand spikes," Toby continued, showing the class Hugo's spiky back.

"Wow!" exclaimed Jack, as the rest of the class gasped.

Hugo lifted his head into the air, looking very proud.

"That's a fantastic fact." Great-Uncle Horace smiled at Toby. "Do you know anything else about them?"

"Yes," replied Toby, his voice growing louder. "Hedgehogs get their name because they like to live in hedges, and they make a grunting noise that sounds a bit like a hog, which is another word for pig."

Hugo gave a little grunt and everyone laughed.

"Show them the picture you drew of Hugo," Zoe said to Toby.

Toby opened his sketch pad and passed it round. As soon as they saw the picture, Zoe's classmates started to clap.

"This is excellent," said Great-Uncle Horace with a twinkly smile.

Both Toby and Hugo looked happier than Zoe had ever seen them, and she gave them her biggest smile.

"I think we should adopt Hugo as our class animal, and not just because he's so interesting," said Toby, looking at the little hedgehog, "but also because he's brand new to the zoo and it can be really hard being new somewhere." Hugo grunted and nuzzled Toby's fingers.

There was a moment's silence and then everyone burst into applause.

"I want to adopt Hugo too," said Jack.

"Me too," said Zoe. "It would be really cool to learn more about hedgehogs."

One by one all her classmates agreed. Even elephant-lover Elliot!

"Well, Toby, I do believe you have achieved the impossible!" Great-Uncle

Horace chuckled. "You've got all your classmates to stop arguing!"

"Let's have a vote," Miss Hawkins suggested. "Raise your hand if you'd like to adopt Hugo the hedgehog as our class animal."

Everyone raised their hands. Hugo, who had scampered up to Toby's shoulder, squeaked in excitement.

Mr Pinch came in. "Why has everyone got their hands in the air?" he asked Zoe.

"We're voting for Hugo the hedgehog to be our adopted class pet."

"Hmm, well, if it keeps him out of mischief, it seems like a very good idea to me," said Mr Pinch, raising his hand.

Just then Sally came out of the kitchen holding a large chocolate cake. It was shaped like a hedgehog, with Smarties for eyes and a mouth and chocolate fingers for spikes. "I didn't want our new arrival to be the only animal without a cake," she said to Zoe with a grin. "So, who would like a piece?"

Seeing the cake, Hugo ran down Toby's arm to the table and sniffed at it. Some of the frosting got on to his nose, and he rolled around the table, trying to get it off. Everyone laughed.

As her friends and Meep gathered at the counter, chatting excitedly, Zoe picked up Hugo and cuddled him. "You see, Hugo?" she whispered. "There was nothing to worry about. You're a part of our zoo family now. You'll have loads of visitors and you'll never be lonely like you were in the woods."

Hugo purred with delight.

"And the best thing is, it's all because you were so helpful!"

Hugo gave a happy squeak.

Zoe, Meep and Hugo all watched the class eat cake and celebrate together at

the party. "What a great day!" Zoe said. "Everyone made new friends – especially you and Toby, Hugo. And now that you're here and settled in, you can help us welcome new animal friends to the Rescue Zoo!"

If you enjoyed Hugo's story,
look out for:

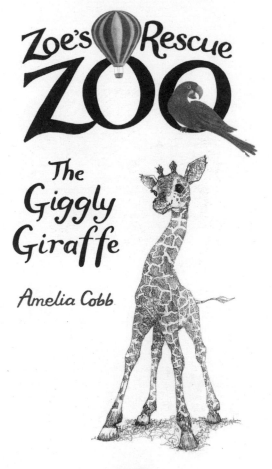

Zoe's Rescue ZOO

The
Giggly
Giraffe

Amelia Cobb

nosy crow

Chapter One
A New Baby

Zoe Parker ran down the red-brick path
of the Rescue Zoo with a huge grin on
her face. "Mum!" she shouted, waving her
arms. "Mum, guess what?"

Lucy Parker popped her head round the
door of the zoo hospital, where she was
working that morning. "I'm here, Zoe!
What's happened?" she asked.

"It's Jewel!" Zoe cried. "Her baby is on the way!"

"That's great news," Lucy smiled. "Wait there, Zoe – I'll be out in just a minute."

Zoe bounced up and down on the path outside the zoo hospital as her mum quickly packed all the things she would need in case she had to help deliver the new baby – a giraffe!

Zoe wasn't just a visitor to the zoo. She actually lived there! Her Great-Uncle Horace had started the zoo a long time ago as a home for any animals that were lost, poorly or in danger. Zoe's mum was the zoo vet, and she and Zoe lived in a cosy little cottage at the edge of the zoo.

Zoe loved her amazing home, and her all-time favourite thing about living in a zoo was when a new animal arrived.

Jewel the giraffe was expecting her first baby, and Zoe had been looking forward to the little calf arriving for such a long time. The other zoo animals were really excited too!

"I'm ready, let's go," said Lucy, stepping outside and swinging a big bag full of special equipment and medicine on to her shoulder.

Together they raced down the path,
past the wolves and the polar bears.
As they passed the pot-bellied pigs, one
of them pushed his snout through a gap
in the fence and gave a grunt. "Yes, the
baby giraffe is coming!" whispered Zoe,
dropping back a little so that her mum
wouldn't hear her. "I'll let you know as

soon as there's any news, Polly!"

Living in the Rescue Zoo wasn't the only special thing about Zoe. She had a very unusual gift – she could talk to animals! It made growing up in a zoo even more fun – although Zoe couldn't let anyone else know her secret. Not even her mum or Great-Uncle Horace knew!

Zoe caught up with her mum again, and when they reached the giraffe enclosure, a tiny furry creature was perched on the gate waiting for them. As soon as he saw Zoe, his fluffy ears pricked up excitedly.

"Hello, Meep," Zoe said as he jumped from the gate on to her shoulder.

Meep was a grey mouse lemur with big golden eyes and a long, curling tail. Of all the animals in the zoo, he was Zoe's most special friend. "I've been keeping an eye on things, Zoe," he chattered importantly. "The baby giraffe hasn't been born yet. But Theo, the giraffe keeper, is here. And someone else has just arrived too," he added happily.

"Someone else? Who do you mean?" asked Zoe, puzzled. "Another zoo keeper?"

Meep shook his head. "Go and look, Zoe," he squeaked.

Zoe followed her mum through the gate and into the giraffe enclosure. She always thought it was one of the nicest parts of the zoo, designed to look just like the African savannah, where giraffes in the wild would live. There were juicy acacia trees dotted around, a gurgling stream winding its way through the middle of the enclosure, and a large watering hole where the giraffes could have a drink and cool down in the summer.

Theo, the Rescue Zoo giraffe keeper, was standing on the other side of the enclosure from Jewel, whose belly was looking very big and round because of the baby inside it. Next to Theo was a man with wild white hair and twinkling brown eyes, wearing dusty safari clothes. On his shoulder perched a beautiful deep-blue bird with a curved black and yellow beak. "Great-Uncle Horace!" gasped Zoe, rushing over to hug him. "I thought you were in Africa."